Ju
F
C34   Chaikin, Miriam.
      I should worry, I
should care.

Temple Israel Library
Minneapolis, Minn.

    Please sign your full name on the above card.

    Return books promptly to the Library or Temple Office.

    Fines will be charged for overdue books or for damage or loss of same.

I Should Worry,
I Should Care

I Should Worry, I Should Care

by Miriam Chaikin

drawings by Richard Egielski

Harper & Row, Publishers
New York, Hagerstown, San Francisco, London

FIRST EDITION

Library of Congress Cataloging in Publication Data
Chaikin, Miriam.
  I should worry, I should care.

  SUMMARY: A young Jewish girl and her family adjust
to a new neighborhood and new friends at a time when the
radio is telling of Hitler's rise to power in Europe.
  [1. Jews in the United States—Fiction. 2. Brooklyn
—Fiction. 3. Family life—Fiction] I. Egielski,
Richard. II. Title
PZ7.C3487Ias   [Fic]   78-19480
ISBN 0-06-021174-1
ISBN 0-06-021175-X lib. bdg.

*For Faye Chaikin Pearl,
my sister Payoo.*

1
The New Apartment

Yesterday, Sunday, Molly and her family moved from the Lower East Side of Manhattan to the Borough Park section of Brooklyn.

Now she stood leaning against the kitchen wall, sucking on her lip and watching her mother unpack. Her mother had been unpacking since after breakfast. But the floor was still covered with barrels and boxes and bundles. There was no room on it even for the kitchen chairs. They were up on the table.

Molly moved out of the way as her mother rolled an empty barrel to the wall. Her mother passed her without a word, then went back to the barrels and started emptying another one. She took out dishes wrapped in newspaper and put them on the table, between the legs of the chairs.

The last stack seemed too close to the edge. Molly was sure it was going to get knocked over. But she was not going to say anything. She had had another argument with her mother at breakfast, and had not spoken since. No one was speaking to her either.

Her father said he'd speak to her when she calmed down. Her mother said she'd speak to her when she behaved like a *mensh.* Joey wasn't talking to her either. But he didn't talk to her even when he was talking, so she couldn't see any difference. Only Rebecca and the baby weren't mad at her. But they were little, and didn't count. Rebecca was only three and a half. She was in the bedroom, napping. And the baby was out on the stoop, in his carriage, getting air.

"You're still leaning on the wall like a coat of paint?" her mother asked suddenly.

Startled, Molly jumped. "There's no place to sit," she said, glad her mother had broken the silence.

"If you would help, instead of standing with your arms folded like a boss, you would have had a place to sit long ago," her mother said.

"I asked you when I came back from the walk if you want me to help. You said no."

Her mother looked at her. "You mean yesterday, after supper, when Papa took you and Joey for a walk around the block to show you the neighborhood?"

Molly nodded.

"After we listened to Eddie Cantor?"

Molly nodded again.

"That was last night," her mother said. "This is today.

We had lunch already. It's after two o'clock. I didn't hear you ask today. . . ."

"You weren't talking to me, so I couldn't say anything," Molly said.

Her mother shoved the dishes further back on the table, to make room for more. "You could have helped me without talking. Here," she said, handing Molly a rag. "Dust!"

"Dust what?" Molly asked.

"Whatever you want," her mother said, leaning over the barrel and sending her arm down into it.

Molly held the rag and looked on. Now that she was talking, she felt the words that had started all the arguments taking shape again. She knew she shouldn't say it, but she couldn't help herself.

"Why did we have to move?" she asked, giving the icebox an angry swipe with the cloth.

Her mother looked up sharply. She took the cloth from Molly and flung it on top of the icebox. "Molly," she said, "don't start up again. I'm warning you. . . ."

Molly glanced away. She knew why they had moved. She had heard the reasons dozens of times: for the same rent, they had an extra room, and Joey could now have his own room; this apartment was on the ground floor—it was easier for Mama to roll the carriage in and out; the ground floor was better for Papa, too, with his heart. She knew all the reasons. But knowing them didn't make her feel any better.

4

Her mother rolled the empty dish barrel out of the way, then took a chair down from the table and put it on the floor.

"Look," she said. "It's beginning to resemble a kitchen."

Molly didn't see where. But she held her tongue. The chair looked inviting and she sidled up to it and sat down—not all the way, just at the edge, so her mother wouldn't think she was making herself at home. She watched her mother put the dishes away in the cupboard.

Seeing the dishes reminded Molly of the old house and a fresh wave of unhappiness washed over her as she thought of the old kitchen, and of Selma and Faigl and her other friends, but especially of Selma and Faigl, her best friends.

"I hate this place," she said under her breath, but loud enough for her mother to hear.

Her mother looked up. "Hate, hate, hate, that's all you know," she said. "You better watch out. The hatred is twisting your face, and you're beginning to look like Mrs. Rappaport."

"Ma!" Molly cried, jumping up. She did not like being compared to Mrs. Rappaport. Her father always said Mrs. Rappaport looked like she was smelling rotten fish.

"Go see for yourself," her mother said, and went back to putting the dishes away.

Molly went into the bathroom and looked in the mirror. She couldn't see any difference. Her face looked the same. Her mother must have made the whole thing up, to scare her. Still, to be on the safe side, she blew out her cheeks to iron out any creases that might be there, then went back to the kitchen.

"Why don't you go out and play?" her mother asked.

Molly stared in amazement. How could her mother be so dumb? "Because I have no one to play with, that's why!" she shouted.

"Shah!" her mother said, putting a finger to her lips. "You'll wake Rebecca." Her mother wet a rag at the sink and wiped a spot off the icebox. "Yesterday you complained it was too hot. Today you have no one to play with. If you go outside," she added, "you'll find someone to play with, you'll make friends."

"I don't want to make friends. I have friends, the best friends in the world," Molly said, thinking of Selma and Faigl, missing them.

"You'll make new friends," her mother said.

"I don't want new friends. I want my old friends back," Molly said, on the point of tears. "I want Selma and Faigl and Beattie and Ruthie. . . ."

"I know . . ." her mother said softly.

"And Skippy . . ." Molly added, seeing that her mother felt sorry for her.

Her mother looked at her. "Skippy? I thought you didn't like Skippy?"

Molly glanced away. It was true. She didn't like

6

Skippy. "That was in the beginning," she said, wondering herself what had made her add Skippy's name.

Her mother scooped up the discarded newspapers and threw them into an empty barrel. A sheet fell on the floor and Molly picked it up, glanced at it, and threw it in after the rest. She wished she had something to read.

"I don't even have a book," she said.

"You'll get one," her mother said.

"Where?"

Her mother looked at her. "Where? From the trees. From the shoemaker. Where does a person get books? From the library, that's where."

"I don't have a card," Molly said.

"You'll get one. Now get out of my way," her mother said, taking a razor blade and scraping paint off the window.

She turned to Molly again. "This morning, Joey didn't know anybody either," she said. "He went outside and met friends, and now he's in the street, playing."

Molly shook her head. How could her mother understand so little? "Boys have it easy," she said. "They don't have friends. All they do is play ball. Friends are different. . . ."

Her mother took a second chair off the table and put it on the floor. Then she took the clothespin bag and went to the kitchen window. She hung the bag on a hook outside the window, then rolled the clothesline across the courtyard, to test it. Molly walked up to the window and looked out. She didn't want to admit it to her mother, but she found the courtyard interesting. She had never seen one before.

"The hook is a little loose," her mother said, jiggling it. "Give me the pliers."

Molly went to the toolbox and took out what she thought were pliers.

"That's the screwdriver," her mother said. "The pliers is the one with two short teeth, like a fat scissors."

Molly found the pliers and handed them to her mother. She tried to look out the window but her mother was blocking her view. She went into Joey's room, off the kitchen, and looked out from his window.

She could see the entire courtyard, and the windows of the two buildings that shared it. She made a count. Two buildings, three floors in each building, two families on each floor. That meant twelve families were living there.

Molly wondered if she shouldn't go outside after all. With all those families, there had to be some children her age for her to play with.

"Go to the front window and see if the baby is all right," her mother called.

Molly crossed the kitchen and went to the living-room window, which looked out on the street. She glanced into the carriage. "He's sleeping," she called back. Her eye was caught by some boys playing ball in an empty lot across the street.

"That does it!" she thought, seeing that one of them was Joey. If he could find kids to play with, she could, too. She decided to go outside and work on her rubber-band ball. Maybe she would see some girls out there. She went into the kitchen to get her ball.

"Ma, I can't find the bag with my ball," she said, looking for it on top of the icebox, where she had left it.

Her mother glanced up from the sink, where she was scrubbing clothes on the washboard. "I moved it before, when the iceman came," she said. "Look on the shelf where the dishes are, under the rags."

Molly found the paper bag which held her ball and a supply of rubber bands and went to the door. She paused, her hand on the knob. She didn't want to go

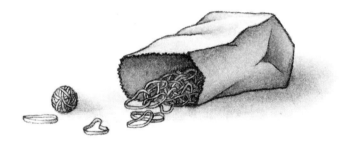

out. She was only going because her mother was forcing her to go. It was cruel, and she felt like punishing her mother.

She knew it made her mother unhappy not to be able

9

to buy new clothes for Rebecca and herself, because they were poor. Everything she and her sister wore came from the rich cousins who lived near the park. Joey got new clothes when he needed them, because there were no boy cousins older than himself in the family.

"I have nothing to wear when school starts," Molly said, rubbing it in.

Her mother looked up from the sink, her hands covered with lather from the brown soap.

"How come you're talking about that now?" she asked.

"I just thought of it," Molly said.

"You'll wear the pink dress."

Molly was disappointed her mother wasn't more bothered by the subject. "Which pink dress?" she asked.

"The one you wore last Rosh Hashanah and that you'll wear again this Rosh Hashanah."

She meant Molly's good-luck dress, the one she wore on test days to bring her luck.

"That's rose, not pink. And it's not new," Molly said.

"The teacher will never notice," her mother said, and went back to her scrubbing.

Molly felt cheated. She wanted to get back at her mother. She knew how to get a rise out of her.

"Okay," she said, "you want me to go out, so I'm going out, but you'll be sorry."

"Why will I be sorry?" her mother asked over her shoulder.

"I might get kidnapped," Molly said. The baby of Charles Lindbergh, the famous flier, had been kidnapped a few years before. All the mothers still talked about it, still worried.

Her mother dried her hands on her apron and came running. "Ptu! Ptu! Ptu!" she said, spitting away the ugly thought. "God forbid!" she said, taking Molly in her arms. "Don't say such a thing, even as a joke!" She gave Molly a kiss, and opened the door.

"Now go," she said, patting her on the behind and shoving her out into the hall.

Molly smiled to herself as she heard the door click shut. Her mother had seemed worried. She turned her head away from the light that streamed in through the glass door that led to the stoop. It was dark in the hall and the light hurt her eyes. Then she squinted at the carriage out on the stoop.

She could not bring herself to go out. Why was her mother forcing her to go out when she didn't know anybody out there? What kind of mother was she? A mother was supposed to take care of her children. Not push them out. Molly sometimes wondered if she was an adopted child. Now she was sure of it. She leaned against the wall about to cry, feeling sorry for herself.

"You're still here?" she heard her mother ask as the apartment door clicked open. "I looked out the window and didn't see you," her mother said.

Molly turned the doorknob. "I had to get my eyes used to the light, didn't I? Do you want me to go blind?" she said.

"Watch the baby," her mother said. "And tell Joey I want him to take the barrels down to the basement."

Feeling her mother's eyes on her back, Molly opened the glass door and went out.

2
The New Block

Molly stood with her hands on the carriage, looking around. She felt guilty. She had hurt her mother, asking about a new dress for school. She promised herself to be extra nice to her mother later. The baby gurgled and she rocked the carriage gently.

Usually she resented having to watch Yaaki, her baby brother. Today she didn't mind. It allowed her to feel busy, as if she were doing something useful, and not like a new girl who had no one to play with. Below her, on the sidewalk, some little kids Rebecca's age were playing. But she saw no one her own age.

Across the street where the boys were playing, Joey hit a ball and ran for a base. His face was red from running. Papa had warned him about playing ball in the heat. He said he might get a sunstroke. The sight of Joey looking so much at home made her feel easier. She let go of the carriage and sat down.

Across the way, in the house directly opposite, a door

opened and a fat lady came out. Molly couldn't believe her eyes. She looked again. The woman was huge, as big as a mountain. Molly wondered if she was from a side show. She had never seen anyone so fat before. The woman lowered herself onto the stoop. She looked over at Molly and smiled.

Embarrassed to be caught staring, Molly half smiled back, then opened her bag and took out her rubber-band ball. She was disappointed to see how skinny it was. She had been working on it for days. Yet she could still see the yellow marble she had started it on showing through. She put a handful of rubber bands in her lap and began adding them to the ball.

As she sat there, the street began to fill. Before long, there were so many people coming and going she put her ball away in the carriage, near the baby's feet, and just watched. The milkman stopped to ask Molly if she was new in the neighborhood. Then he went inside to talk to her mother about delivering milk. Then the man who sharpened knives and scissors came and people brought him things to sharpen. Molly watched the sparks fly as his wheel spun around.

Molly sat up. To her great delight, the fruit man brought his horse and wagon to a stop in front of her house. She jumped off the stoop and went to stand near the horse. Close, but not too close. One of the women who was buying plums fed the horse a lump of sugar from her hand. Molly marveled at the woman's nerve.

She couldn't even bring herself to touch the horse.

As she glanced up, she noticed two girls on the next stoop. That was the house that shared her courtyard. Wouldn't it be wonderful to have those girls as friends! Molly felt a rush of excitement. But standing here, among the women, she might be hidden. And she wanted the girls to see her. She ran back and sat down on the stoop, where she could be seen.

The girls looked at her, then whispered to each other. When they came walking toward her, she was sure they were going to speak. But they didn't. They crossed the street and went up to the fat lady's house and stood on the sidewalk looking up at her. Molly watched them, wondering what they were up to.

"Fat Anna! Fat Anna!" they yelled suddenly, then ran away laughing.

Upstairs, a white-haired woman came to the window. "Get outta here, rotten kids!" she cried, shaking a fist at them.

Molly was shocked. Children making fun of a grown-up? What kind of girls could they be? And the fat woman, what was wrong with her? She didn't yell back, or run after them, or anything. She just sat there, smiling.

The baby began to cry and Molly ran up the steps. Her mother came to the window.

"Did I hear the baby cry?" her mother asked.

"He's sleeping now," Molly said, rocking the carriage.

"Rebecca's up. I'll wash her face and send her out. Watch her, please," her mother said.

Molly could have spit. What a life she had! She hated the place where she lived. She had no friends. She was stuck watching the baby. And now she had to watch her sister, too.

"I thought Lincoln freed the slaves," she said, giving the carriage an angry shake.

"Molly! The baby!" her mother cried.

Molly felt like a crumb, taking it out on the poor baby. She shook the carriage more gently.

"Be a good girl, and God will reward you," her mother said, and left the window.

Molly felt tears rising in her eyes. She never knew it was possible to be so miserable. If only God *would* reward her. She looked heavenward. "Please, God, give me back my friends Selma and Faigl. Or even only Selma," she said, and began to cry. As she turned to the house to hide her tears, she saw Rebecca through the glass door and quickly looked away.

She could hear Rebecca rattling the door, trying to get it open, but she ignored her so she could blink away her tears and straighten her face.

At last, Rebecca got the door open.

Molly turned to her sister. The scrap of old blanket she always carried was in her hand.

"Why didn't you help me?" Rebecca asked.

"How are you ever going to learn anything if I have

16

to keep helping you all the time?" Molly asked.

Rebecca did not respond. She had noticed the children playing on the sidewalk. Shuffling over to the side, so she could hold on, she hurried down the steps of the stoop one foot at a time.

Watching her sister sit down with the children, Molly felt sorry for herself all over again. Joey had friends. Rebecca had friends. What about her? She was on the verge of breaking out into tears when she noticed the same two girls walking back toward her. Molly didn't like them. She didn't want to have anything to do with them. All the same, she wondered if this time they would stop and speak to her.

They went up the steps of the next house without so much as glancing her way. One girl looked up and seemed about to say something, but the other opened the door and yanked her inside.

"Twerps!" Molly said to herself. "Nitwits! Creeps! They stink to high heaven!" She thought of her wonderful friends Selma and Faigl, and her eyes filled with tears. Life was not worth living without friends. She glanced at the sky, then closed her eyes. "Dear God, help me," she said. "Give me a friend. Please, God, hurry. . . ."

When she opened her eyes, she saw her father coming down the street. She wondered if God had misunderstood her. She had asked for a *friend*, not a *relative*. She was about to close her eyes again, to state her wish more clearly, but when she saw her father wave, she changed her mind.

She waved back, glad to see that he wasn't mad anymore. Joey left his game and ran across to join Papa. They came walking toward the house, Joey bouncing his ball. Papa stopped where the children were playing and gave Rebecca a kiss.

"Well, Molly," Papa said, standing before her. "How do you like the new block? It's nice, huh, with the trees?"

Molly was glad enough to wave to him. But she didn't want him to get the idea that she was happy or anything. "I don't see any trees," she said, looking where there were none.

"Dummy!" Joey said. "Don't you know a tree when you see one?"

Papa went up the stoop to look in the carriage. When his back was turned, Molly stuck her tongue out at her brother.

"Double dummy," Joey said, and began throwing the ball against the steps of the stoop. The ball came nowhere near Molly, but she ducked as if it had.

"Pa!" Molly cried. "Make him stop!"

Papa turned around. "Joey, the ball can hit somebody," he said.

Joey held the ball up in front of his mouth like a microphone and sang, "Nobody loves me, I wonder why, I wonder why that should be."

18

"Pa!" Molly cried, glaring at her brother.

Papa spun around and gave each of them a sharp look. "Children! That's enough!" he said.

Mama came to the window. "Avram, I thought I heard your voice," she said. "I need a couple of things from Thirteenth Avenue. But first bring in the baby. I want to change him."

"I want to go, too, Pa," Molly said. At least it would take her away from the crummy stoop for a while, she thought.

Mama looked at Joey. "I want you to take the barrels down to the basement—didn't Molly tell you?"

"I forgot," Molly said.

"She didn't forget," Joey said. "Her tongue got sunburned hanging out, she couldn't speak."

"All right, that's enough," Mama said.

Papa took the baby out of the carriage and carried him inside. Joey gave the ball a hard bounce in front of Molly's face as he ran by. To spite him, she didn't flinch.

With everyone gone, Molly felt terribly alone. That was a new feeling for her. She never used to feel alone, not in the old neighborhood where they used to live. She wished she had someone to talk to.

Aside from the children playing on the sidewalk, the only one around was the fat lady across the street. Molly decided to go and talk to her. She could still keep an eye on Rebecca from there, in case the kidnapper came. She jumped down from the stoop.

"Rebecca," she called.

Rebecca came walking over, holding the rag in her mouth.

"See that lady?" Molly said, pointing across the street.

Rebecca nodded.

"I'm going across to talk to her. I'll watch you from there. Do you remember the rules?"

Rebecca nodded.

"What are they?"

Rebecca took the rag out of her mouth. "Don't go near the gutter. And don't talk to strangers."

"And?" Molly said.

"And don't take anything from a stranger," Rebecca said, and stuck the rag back in her mouth again.

Molly went to the curb and looked both ways to make sure no cars were coming, then crossed over. She stood before the fat lady and arranged herself so she could talk to her and keep an eye on Rebecca at the same time.

"Hi," Molly said, looking up.

The fat lady turned to Molly. She had short black chopped-off hair. Molly had to hide her surprise. The lady was even fatter close up. Each of her arms was as big as a person. Molly noticed that the lady's dress was dirty. But she didn't care. At least she had someone to talk to.

Molly nodded across the street. "We just moved in. I live over there," she said. "The little girl with the rag

in her mouth is my sister."

The lady smiled.

"Anna!" a voice called from above.

Molly looked up. The old woman with the white hair was leaning out the window.

"Anna, come up. It's time to eat," she said.

Molly found the situation strange. The fat lady looked too old to have a mother. And the mother treated her like a child.

Anna got up. There was a little pocket sewn on her dress. She took a stick of gum out of it and handed it to Molly.

"Thanks," Molly said, as Anna went inside. She inspected the gum. It was bent and dirty, but the inside wrapper was clean. She tore off the wrapper, popped the gum into her mouth, and went back across the street.

She could have kicked herself when she saw Rebecca walking toward her. She should have had sense enough not to chew in front of Rebecca. Her sister was only three and a half but she didn't miss a thing.

"I want gum, too," Rebecca said.

"I don't have any more," Molly said.

"I'm going to tell Mama you took gum from a stranger."

Molly could have smacked her sister. She knew that's what she would say. "That's no stranger, stupid," she said. "She lives right there, in that house. It was only half a piece, anyhow," she added.

"Let me see," Rebecca said.

Molly bit the gum in two and hid half under her tongue. She pulled out the other half and showed it to Rebecca. Rebecca looked it over and went back to her friends.

Molly felt victorious. It wasn't often that she was able to outsmart her sister. Molly sat down on the stoop and took care to chew only when Rebecca wasn't looking.

She sat up suddenly. One of the girls was coming out of the house next door. Molly looked away. She was not going to get caught acting stupid again. The next thing she knew, the girl was standing in front of her.

"Hi," the girl said.

"Oh, hi," Molly said, pretending she hadn't noticed her until now.

"You just moved in?" the girl asked.

Molly nodded. "My name's Molly. What's yours?"

"Mine's Julie," the girl said.

"Do you live in that house?" Molly asked.

"No, Lynn lives there. I live around the corner, on Thirteenth Avenue."

"My father took me and my brother for a walk around the block yesterday. I was on Thirteenth Avenue," Molly said, glad to talk to someone her own age.

"I live over the tailor store," Julie said. "I have to go home now and help my mother. She has high blood pressure. She's always sick. I don't want her to worry

23

about me. See you later," she said, and walked off.

Molly liked Julie. She seemed nice. She couldn't imagine how such a nice girl could have made fun of Fat Anna. As she watched her go, she forgot and popped her gum.

"Selfish!" Rebecca called.

Molly pretended she hadn't heard. A potsy had been drawn on the sidewalk and she jumped down and began hopping across the squares.

"Molly!" her mother called from the window.

Molly went up to the window.

Her mother threw some coins wrapped in a handkerchief onto the sidewalk.

"I want you to go to Thirteenth Avenue for me. Papa's tired," her mother said.

Molly was surprised. "All alone?" she asked, picking up the hanky. She couldn't believe she had heard right. Her mother was sending her out shopping. By herself. In a new neighborhood. Molly fiddled with the knot, then counted out the change.

"Fifteen cents," she said.

"Thirteenth Avenue is that way," her mother said, pointing down the street.

"Ma! I know that!" Molly said.

"You remember the stores Papa showed you?"

Molly nodded.

"Go to the dairy and buy a container of sour cream. Next door is a bakery. Get a rye bread, with seeds. And don't let him slice it."

Molly tried not to let her excitement show, but she was jumping inside. Going shopping alone was a big thing. It was also scary. What if she got lost? What if she couldn't find the store? What if she saw a kidnapper?

"You'll have two cents change," her mother said. "Take Rebecca with you. Buy a sour pickle with the change, and give her half."

Molly didn't want Rebecca tagging along. She was about to protest, then changed her mind. If she got lost, she could blame it on her sister.

Rebecca came running over. "Mama said to take me," she said.

"Well, come on," Molly said, heading for Thirteenth Avenue. "What do you want me to do, carry you?"

"Wait for me," Rebecca called, hurrying after her.

Molly waited for her sister to catch up. Rebecca took her hand and they walked on together. As they passed a hedge, Molly spit out her gum. She might forget and start chewing. It wasn't worth the risk, with Rebecca around.

They passed the same houses she had seen yesterday, then the shoe store, and the Chinese laundry, and then, near the corner, the synagogue.

Molly felt a growing sense of excitement. She was walking down the street alone—almost. And she might run into Julie. Even if she didn't, she would see where Julie lived.

As they got close to Thirteenth Avenue, Molly felt an explosion of happiness inside her. Whenever she felt that way, she skipped and sang her happiness song. Now, with Rebecca holding on to her, she couldn't skip. But she could sing. She had a way of doing it so no one could hear. And, pressing her lips together, she sang joyfully under her breath:

"I should worry, I should care,
I should marry a millionaire."

3
The Courtyard

As they reached the corner, Molly clasped Rebecca's hand more firmly. The avenue was crowded with shoppers. The pushcarts, lined up one after the other, made a little wall on the gutter side of the street. They were stacked high with fruits, vegetables, nuts, shoelaces, hats, everything. On the other side of the street were stores. Merchandise hung from awnings and was set out on tables in front of the stores. Above the stores were windows.

Molly looked up. Julie lived behind one of those windows.

"Molly, look," Rebecca said, marveling at what she saw.

"I saw it already, when I went with Papa," Molly said, feeling superior.

She felt safe as she made her way down the avenue, stepping between the people, looking for the dairy. She didn't have to be afraid of kidnappers here. Not with so many people around.

"Here's the dairy," Rebecca said, tugging at Molly's hand.

Molly had already noticed it. But she was looking for the tailor shop, so she could see Julie's windows. "Just a minute, I want to see something first," she said. There it was, a few doors down, the tailor shop, and above, some windows painted green.

"Come on," Rebecca said.

They went into the dairy and bought sour cream. The bakery was next door. There was a short line and they had to wait.

Molly sniffed. "Doesn't it smell good?" she said to Rebecca. "Should we buy two cents' worth of cookies, instead of a pickle?"

"No, I want a pickle," Rebecca said.

Irritated, Molly stepped up to the counter to take her turn and asked for a rye bread with seeds, unsliced. When she received the bread, she was glad Rebecca had insisted on the pickle. They would be almost through eating their cookies by now. As it was, they still had the pickle to look forward to.

"Give me something to carry," Rebecca said as they stepped outside.

Molly gave her the bread. It was heavier than the sour cream, but it wouldn't make a mess if she dropped it.

As they made their way through the crowd looking for the sour-pickle lady, Molly kept watching for Julie, hoping to see her.

"There's the sour pickles," Rebecca said, letting go of Molly's hand and running off.

"Come back this minute!" Molly yelled. The thought of her sister getting lost, even momentarily, sent her into a panic.

No one in the family knew why, but Rebecca was terrified of a bloody nose. "You want to get a bloody nose?" Molly said, trying to scare her sister into obeying her. Rebecca stood frozen in her tracks, waiting for Molly to catch up. She grabbed Rebecca's hand and pulled her over to the pickle barrel.

The smell made Molly's mouth water as she stood looking over the mass of pickles bobbing about.

"Vatta ya vant, sveethott?" the pickle lady said.

"A two-cent pickle, please," Molly said, holding up her money.

The lady picked out one of the smaller pickles and gave it to her.

Molly pulled Rebecca off to a side, where it was less crowded, and gave her the other bag to hold while she broke the pickle in two. Knowing her sister, she was extra careful to divide it as evenly as possible.

"Here," she said, giving Rebecca half.

Rebecca looked at it. "Yours is bigger," she said.

Molly could have spit. "They're both the same," she said, and yanked the bags away from her sister. "Now shut up and eat your pickle!" Molly leaned forward, so the pickle juice wouldn't drip on her, and bit in.

She felt good, being on her own, taking care of her

little sister. She looked around, curious about the rest of the neighborhood. She had been around the whole block, last night with her father. But she was too mad at the time to notice anything.

"Do you want to see Forty-second Street?" she asked her sister.

"No," Rebecca said, pickle juice dripping down all over her.

"Well, I do. Come on," Molly said, finishing her pickle.

She turned up the street, with Rebecca following. When they were halfway up the block, Molly was sorry she had chosen to go that way. It was longer. They had been gone for some time now. Her mother might be worried that they weren't back.

"Let's hurry," she said.

They passed a houseful of furniture that had been set out on the sidewalk. Two children were sitting on top of a rolled-up mattress.

"Can I play with them?" Rebecca asked.

"No," Molly said, shoving her sister along. "They're not playing. They were dispossessed."

"What's that?" Rebecca asked.

"They couldn't pay the rent, and the landlord threw them out," Molly said.

Rebecca wiped her hands on her dress. "When are we going to get home?" she asked.

"Two more corners," Molly said.

"I'm tired," Rebecca complained.

"We'll soon be home," Molly said.

As they turned the corner to Fourteenth Avenue, Molly's heart gave a leap. The big red building on the other side of the street was P.S. 164, the school she would be going to in September. Joey, too. For his last term. Papa had pointed it out last night. She had forgotten about it until this moment. She could hardly wait for school to begin.

The thought of school also frightened her. The other girls would all know each other. They would all be friends. She was new, and wouldn't know anyone.

"What are you looking at?" Rebecca asked.

"That's the school I'm going to go to," she said.

"Me, too?" Rebecca asked.

"You're still too young."

As they walked along, Molly suddenly grabbed Rebecca's hand and rushed her past the missionary store they were passing. Molly hadn't noticed it last night. Neither had her father. Maybe it was closed. Now the door was wide open. Molly knew what it was from the crosses and the Bibles in the window. Missionaries hated Jews. They stole Jewish children and made Gentiles out of them. Molly didn't want her sister to see it and get scared. She started talking, to keep Rebecca from noticing.

"I'll still be in that school when you start kindergarten," she said. "I'll be able to take you to school in the morning. When I graduate from there, I go to Montauk Junior High School. Papa said it's two blocks away."

Molly kept talking, saying whatever came into her mind. She was relieved to find herself at the corner. They were both surprised to see a candy store.

"I didn't know this was here," Molly said. "We could have bought licorice or gum instead of a sour pickle."

"Then why did you make me get a pickle?" Rebecca said.

Molly dropped her sister's hand. "I made you get a pickle?" she said.

"You wanted the pickle," Rebecca said.

Molly glared at her sister. "You are some liar!" she said. "The way you're going, you'll be in jail by the time you're seven years old. I don't want to walk with liars."

Molly turned the corner and hurried down Forty-third Street. She saw her mother leaning out the window and rushed up to her.

"Where were you so long?" her mother asked. "I was getting worried."

"It's her fault," Molly said, nodding toward Rebecca. "Look how she crawls."

"Why are you coming from that direction? Thirteenth Avenue is the other way."

"I wanted to see the whole neighborhood," Molly said. "Ma," she added excitedly, "I saw the school—"

"Ma," Rebecca said, arriving at the window. "The people who hate Jews have a store around the corner.

32

Molly didn't want me to see it, but I saw it anyhow."

Molly glared at her sister.

Mama turned to Molly. "What was there?"

"A missionary store," Molly said. "I didn't want her to see it and get scared. I was trying to protect her—"

"I don't want you to go near there," Mama said.

"Me?" Molly said. "You better talk to her." She turned to Rebecca. "I tried to protect you, and the whole time you knew it was there. Boy! I'm never taking you anyplace again."

"What did I do?" Rebecca asked.

"All right, never mind, children," Mama said. "Come in. Supper is ready."

Molly and Rebecca went inside. Molly was surprised to see how nice the house looked. Joey had taken all the empty barrels and boxes down to the basement. The floor was clear. The chairs were around the table. And the kitchen looked like the kitchen in the old house.

The living room looked nice, too. Papa was sitting on the couch, playing with the baby. Joey was sitting in the easy chair, reading.

"All right, wash hands, everyone," Mama said.

Molly and Rebecca washed their hands at the kitchen sink and Joey went into the bathroom. Mama brought sour cream to the table and cut bananas up onto everyone's plate. Molly and Rebecca sat down at the table. Papa joined them and put on his skullcap.

"Where's Joey?" Papa asked.

33

Mama held the bread up to her chest, slicing it with a knife. "He'll be right out," she said.

Papa started humming.

Molly was annoyed. She was hungry and wanted to eat. But she couldn't start until her father said the blessing. And he wouldn't say it until Joey came to the table. Nothing ever got started without Joey. And all because he was a boy.

"At last!" Molly said, as her brother came to the table. She saw him make a face at his plate as he sat down.

Papa said the blessing. *"Bo-ruch a-toh Ado-nai—* Blessed art thou, O Lord," he began, thanking God for the gift of food.

"Amen," everyone answered.

"Bananas and cream again?" Joey said. "We had the same thing for lunch!"

Molly gave her brother a dirty look. She sometimes wondered if *he* was adopted. He had no feelings.

"So? What's wrong with that?" Papa said. "I could eat it three times a day. It's delicious. In Europe, we felt lucky when we ate bananas and cream."

Molly glanced away, irritated with her father for being so soft on her brother. He should have sent him away from the table for being so fresh.

"We had strawberries, not bananas, for lunch," Mama said. She buttered a piece of bread and gave it to Rebecca. "I suppose I didn't have enough to do today, without cooking?" she said, staring at the bread but talking to Joey.

34

Molly glared at her brother. "Uuuuu! Are you selfish! Mama worked like a slave all day," she said.

"Leave him alone, Molly," Mama said.

Molly smacked her spoon down on the table. She couldn't believe that she actually heard her mother sticking up for Joey. "Excuse me for living," she said. "I was only trying to help you. . . ."

Mama reached over and pulled her face over to give her a kiss. "You did help," she said. "You took care of the children. You went shopping. You were a regular angel."

Molly felt tears welling up in her eyes. She didn't want her brother to see, so she blinked and looked away.

"Some angel," Joey said.

"Joey, be careful," Mama said. "Or I'll send you away from the table."

Glad to hear Joey scolded, Molly picked up her spoon and continued eating.

"Am I an angel, too?" Rebecca asked.

Mama wiped butter from Rebecca's chin. "All my children are angels," she said. "Every one of you."

"The baby, too?" Rebecca asked.

"Especially the baby. He sleeps all the time," Mama said with a laugh. She took a bite of bread. "Tomorrow I'll make salmon *latkes*—everybody likes that. Wednesday I'll make cheese *blintzes*. Thursday I don't know—but Mrs. Mason, the lady upstairs, told me there's a big poultry market on Thirteenth Avenue. I'll go in the morning, before the day gets too hot, and get a nice chicken for *Shabbos*."

Molly looked up. Her mother had a friend, too.

"Does Mrs. Mason have any children?" she asked.

"She has a son in high school," Mama said. "Too old even for Joey."

"I thought you didn't like bananas and cream," Molly said, watching her brother shovel his food in.

"I don't," he said. "I'm making believe it's meat and potatoes."

"Ma, can I go with you to the market?" Rebecca asked. "I want to see them pull the feathers out of the chickens."

"Sure," Mama said.

The thought of the smell of the chicken market made Molly nauseous. "Pu! It stinks in there," she said, holding her nose. "You couldn't pay me to go."

"I didn't hear anybody invite you," Joey said.

"When I ask for toilet paper, you can roll out!" Molly cried.

"Children! That's enough!" Mama said.

Papa looked up. "You heard Mama. That's enough!"

Molly gave Joey a dirty look and went back to eating. It was silent around the table. She could hear the voices of two women talking in the courtyard. Their voices died away and a few moments later a man's voice arose, crying, "I cash clothes! I cash clothes!"

Molly got up and ran to the window. A man with a

pack strapped to his back stood waiting to see if anyone answered his call.

"I cash clothes!" he repeated.

A woman in an upstairs window beckoned to him to come up. As the woman moved away from the window, Molly saw Lynn.

"Hi!" Molly called, delighted to see someone she knew and forgetting that she didn't like her.

Lynn waved, then moved away, and Molly went back to the table.

"That was my friend Lynn," Molly said.

"Lynn?" Joey asked. "Where did she get such a fancy name? Only movie stars have names like that."

Molly didn't answer. It wasn't exactly true that Lynn was her friend. But she didn't want to be the only one in the family who hadn't made a new friend. Julie was a new friend, sort of, but Lynn was there to talk about and Julie wasn't. Molly poured herself a glass of milk and took a chocolate-covered doughnut from the box on the table.

Mama brought Papa a glass of tea, with a cube of sugar in the saucer. "You see?" she said. "I told you, if you went out, you would meet friends."

Molly didn't bother saying anything. No one would understand. Lynn wasn't her friend yet. But she would be. Even if Molly didn't like her.

The sounds of a fiddle came from the courtyard and everyone looked up. Someone was playing "Play, Fiddle, Play," Mama's favorite song. She always cried when she heard it on the radio.

"Ma, do you hear what they're playing?" Molly said, and ran to the window.

"I hear, I hear," Mama said, getting up and going to the window. Rebecca went, too, and Mama, Molly, and Rebecca sat huddled in the window, listening to the song. Molly had heard a violin being played before, but only on the radio. She had never seen a real live person play.

"Ma," she said softly, enjoying the moment. "A concert, right under our window. . . ."

Mama nodded, and brushed a tear from her eye. "I heard about such a thing, but I never saw it before," she said.

Molly knew her mother was crying because she felt good. And that made her feel good, too. She glanced up at Lynn's windows, but they were dark. When the violinist finished playing, people threw him pennies from the windows. Mama got a penny and also threw him one.

"Very nice," Mama said, as they all returned to the table.

Molly finished her milk in silence. She wanted to hold on to the nice feeling she had. Everyone seemed to feel the same way. Even Joey. He hummed a little tune as Papa drummed on the table and sipped his tea through the piece of sugar in his mouth.

After supper, Joey did the dishes. Usually Molly washed and he dried. But tonight he said he was giving her the night off. He sometimes did things like that. Molly was grateful to him.

Papa changed the baby's diaper and put him to sleep. And Mama got Rebecca ready for bed.

It was a hot night and Molly took a shower to cool off. Then she got into her pajamas and sat down at the kitchen table, where Papa sat listening to the radio, waiting for the news to come on. Joey, in pajamas, came in from his room and sat down, too.

Benny Goodman's band came on playing "Begin the Beguine." Molly worked on her ball as she listened. It was tuneful and made her want to sing along, and she began to sing aloud, but it was a hard melody and she kept hitting the wrong notes. When she caught the look on her brother's face, she stopped herself. Then the news came on: "Good evening, this is Gabriel Heatter. The news is bad tonight."

Everyone sat up. Mama left the baby and came in from the living room to listen. They all waited to hear what the news would be. Europe was at war. Hitler, the mad ruler of Germany, had conquered country after country. He wanted to kill all the Jews. Wherever his soldiers went, they arrested Jews and sent them to concentration camps. No one ever heard from them again. One night, Walter Winchell said on the radio that all the Jews of Vienna had been rounded up and sent to camps in Poland.

Gabriel Heatter first gave the American news. A lot of people were out of work in the cities and the farmers were suffering because there was no rain to water the crops. Then he gave the world news. Mama, resting a hand on the table, leaned closer to listen: "The persecution of the Jews continues. New laws in Vichy France force Jews to sell their businesses and turn the money over to the government. Hungary expels Jewish refugees fleeing for their lives, and Rumania admits that Jews were killed in a pogrom there early in the year."

Mama pressed her fingers into the table. Her knuckles were white. Papa bit his lips. "Nobody lifts a finger to help," he said. "In the whole world, no country cares what happens to the Jews. . . ."

Joey got up and left the table.

As always when she heard these reports, Molly was upset. She knew there were people in America who were against the Jews. Father Coughlin, in Detroit, hated Jews and told lies about them on the radio. But

Hitler wanted to kill all the Jews.

Molly thought about President Roosevelt. He was a powerful man. Why couldn't the President of the United States stop Hitler? Why couldn't he help the Jews? Why couldn't God?

After the news, there was a concert. Molly didn't feel like listening to it. She said good night and went into the living room. Her room, the room where she slept with Rebecca, was next to it. But the living room looked so nice she paused to glance around. How different it was from this morning. Now the curtains were up. The baby was sleeping quietly in his crib. And the couch hadn't yet been opened up into the bed where Mama and Papa slept. The cozy and orderly look of the living room made Molly feel good.

She tiptoed into the bedroom. Rebecca was curled up on her side of the bed. It was hot and she had kicked the covers off. Trying not to wake her sister, Molly got into bed and lay quietly, thinking.

She thought about Selma and Faigl, and cried softly to herself at how much she missed them. Then Lynn and Julie came to her mind. Lynn looked like a pill. But Julie had seemed nice. Molly wondered why Julie should have made fun of the fat lady. She wondered if she would see Lynn tomorrow. And how she would act. And if she would see Julie. And if the fat lady would be sitting there again, in the same place.

Molly began to look forward to the morning. She

turned on her side. Her sister looked so cuddly, lying there, Molly could have hugged her. Instead, she snuggled up to her and lightly put an arm over her. Rebecca didn't feel it.

After a while, Molly removed her arm, turned over, and fell asleep.

4
The Schoolyard

The next morning, Molly could hardly wait to go out.
Each time she started for the door, her mother called
her back to do something else. Now she stood at the
kitchen sink, heating the baby's bottle under the hot
water. To rush it, she opened the faucet still more, and
turned the bottle round and round. Her mother had
already sent her back to the sink once, saying the bottle
wasn't hot enough. Now Molly touched it again, and
thought it was.

She brought it into the living room, where her
mother was diapering the baby.

"Try it, it's plenty hot now," Molly said, holding the
bottle up for her mother to touch.

"Put it down," her mother said, talking through the
safety pins in her mouth.

Molly rested the bottle against the arm of the couch.
Then, before her mother could think of something else
for her to do, she went to the kitchen, got her ball bag,
and ran to the door.

"Don't go far," her mother called after her.

"I won't," Molly said.

In the hall, she stepped around Rebecca and another little girl, playing on the floor, and went out.

She saw Anna sitting across the street, and called to her. Anna smiled back. Anna seemed always to be smiling. Molly sat down on the stoop facing Lynn's house, so she could see her when she came out. She wondered about Lynn. Maybe she had been wrong about her. Last night, when she waved from the window, she seemed really nice. Molly wondered if she would snub her again today, or if she would talk to her.

She took out her ball and looked at it. The yellow hardly showed through anymore. It was definitely getting bigger. She put a supply of rubber bands in her lap and began adding them to the ball.

Before long the door of the next house opened and Lynn was standing on the stoop. She was holding a jump rope. She saw Molly and waved. Glad to be greeted, Molly waved back. She watched Lynn go down the steps and start jumping rope. As she jumped, she said, loud enough for Molly to hear:

"I won't go to Macy's any more, more, more.
There's a big fat policeman at the door, door, door.
He grabs you by the collar,
And makes you pay a dollar.
I won't go to Macy's any more, more, more."

45

Show-off, Molly thought.

Lynn folded her rope and came over to Molly.

"I saw you from the window last night," she said.

"I know. I saw you, too," Molly said, glad Lynn had come up to her. "We just moved in, on Sunday," she added.

"Is Joey your brother?"

Molly nodded, wondering how Lynn knew about Joey.

"I saw him playing ball yesterday. How old is he?"

"Eleven and a half," Molly said.

"What's your name?" Lynn asked.

"Molly." Molly smiled. "I know yours. It's Lynn."

The girl looked surprised. "Who told you that?"

"Julie," Molly said.

"My real name is Celia. Only Julie is allowed to call me Lynn. She has to. I told her to. She does everything I tell her. I'm her best friend."

Molly wondered if that's why Julie made fun of Anna yesterday. She considered it as she watched Celia turn to look at a man and woman walking toward her house. It was morning. Yet they were both all dressed up. Celia ran up to them, said something to the woman, and handed her the rope.

"Is that your mother and father?" Molly asked when Celia came back.

"My father's dead. That's the boarder," Celia said. "I know him since I'm a baby." She picked up a little stone

46

someone had left in the potsy and threw it in the gutter. "I'm going over to Julie's house. Want to come?" she asked.

Molly's heart did a flip-flop. Did she ever? "Wait. I'll tell my mother," she said, jumping up.

Celia laughed. "Tell your mother? What are you, a baby? I don't have to tell my mother anything. I'm my own boss. She never knows where I am."

Molly resented being called a baby. But Celia was tough. And if she answered her back, she might get mad and go away without her. So she didn't say anything.

"Ma!" Molly called into the open window.

Her mother appeared.

"I'm going with Ly— with Celia to Julie's house," Molly said.

Her mother looked Celia over. "Hello, Celia. Where does Julie live?"

"Around the corner."

"And where do you live, dear?"

"Next door," Celia said, pointing with her chin. "I can see you from my window."

Molly saw the look of surprise on her mother's face. "Is that so?" her mother asked. She turned to Molly. "Okay, go, but don't be gone long. And let me see you when you get back."

Molly loved her mother that moment. She could have squeezed and squeezed her. Her mother hadn't told her how long to stay away, or by what time to be back. Celia couldn't say she was treated like a baby. Molly went up to the window, leaned over, and handed her mother her ball bag to take inside. Then she went down the steps to join Celia.

Molly felt a stab in her chest when she saw Celia standing at the curb and staring across at Anna.

"Watch this," Celia said.

Molly was afraid to look.

"Anna!" Celia yelled across the street.

The moment Anna looked up, Celia stuck her thumbs in her ears and, wiggling her fingers, cried, "Koo-Koo! Fat Anna!"

Molly turned away. "You shouldn't do that," she said, feeling disgusted.

Celia laughed. "She doesn't care. She's crazy. You do it, too. Come on!"

Molly was shocked. "I don't want to," she said.

Celia stared at her. "If you want to be my friend, you better do it," she said. "I'll let you off easy," she added. "If you don't want to say anything, just make a face."

Molly didn't want to obey Celia. But so far, she had no other friends. Quickly, Molly glanced across the street.

"There," she said. "I did it."

"I didn't see you."

"I can't help it, I did it anyhow," Molly said.

Celia seemed satisfied, and walked off toward Thirteenth Avenue. Molly caught up with her.

Molly was curious about what Celia had said before. "You mean your mother never knows where you are?" she said.

"I'm independent," Celia said.

Molly wasn't sure she knew what that meant.

"My mother raised me to be independent," Celia added. "She's not home much, because she works. And she says a girl has to learn how to look out for herself."

Molly didn't know what to say. She had never met anyone like Celia before. She was glad when they reached Thirteenth Avenue. She was looking forward to seeing Julie again.

"Julie told me yesterday she lived over the tailor store. That must be her house over there," Molly said, nodding at the green painted windows as if she didn't know.

"It is," Celia said.

They stopped in front of the tailor store.

"Ju-lie!" Celia yelled, looking up.

Molly was glad to see Julie appear. "Hi," she said.

Julie smiled back.

"Come on out," Celia said. "We're going to the schoolyard."

"I can't. My mother doesn't feel good. I have to stay home," Julie said.

"Tough!" Celia said. "Maybe we'll see you later." She put an arm around Molly, but Molly knew she was only doing it to make Julie jealous. "Come on," Celia said, pulling Molly along.

Molly felt sorry for Julie, and wished she were coming, too. But at least she had seen her again. That was something. Now she could go to Julie's house again—without Celia. And Julie could come see her, too.

"So long," Molly called over her shoulder as Celia dragged her away.

"Her mother gives me a pain," Celia said. "She makes believe she's sick, so Julie can't go out. That dumb Julie doesn't even know it."

Molly had never heard of a mother making believe she didn't feel good. "How could a mother do that?" she asked.

"My mother says Julie's father ran away. Now her mother makes believe she's sick so Julie will feel sorry for her and stay home with her," Celia said. "They're on home relief," she added. "My mother saw her mother shopping with food coupons."

Molly was hearing a lot of strange things for the first time. She didn't like Celia. But she had to admit that Celia knew a lot.

Celia let go of her and started running, and as Molly ran after her it occurred to her to ask, "Why are we going to the schoolyard anyhow?"

"To summer school. Why'd you think?"

Molly stopped. Summer school? She had never been to summer school before. The school where she used to

50

live didn't have a summer program. She thought she ought to go home and tell her mother where she was going. But Celia would only call her a baby again. She decided to forget about it.

"Hey!" Celia said, turning around to see where she was.

"I'm coming," Molly said, running to catch up.

When Molly set foot in the schoolyard, she saw a different world. Yesterday she had thought that in all the neighborhood there were only two kids her age. But the schoolyard was full of them. Everywhere she looked, groups of children of all ages were running and skating and playing games—boys and girls alike.

Celia introduced Molly to Mrs. Rice, who was in charge. She was the gym teacher of the regular school, too. And she was wearing the regular green gym suit. Molly had one, too. Mrs. Rice brought Molly over to some girls who were jumping double Dutch, and Molly joined in. Before the morning was over, in addition to jumping rope and playing potsy, Molly had played basketball with the girls and come in second in a bean-bag race. Celia had come in third. Suddenly, she started limping and saying she would have come in first if she didn't have a sprained ankle. But Molly had seen no sign of a sprained ankle earlier. Molly was glad she had decided to run. At first she wasn't even going to try. But Mrs. Rice had talked her into it.

Great as the games were, the best thing about the

morning was meeting Norma and Lily and Esther and Shami and the two Naomis. Molly had been in games with all of them, and she liked them all. Norma was quiet. She was quieter than the others. For some reason, Molly liked her best.

Molly left the schoolyard with Celia and Norma. Every now and then she lagged behind to see if Celia was still limping. Sometimes she was, and sometimes she wasn't.

"Hey, guess what," Celia said as they crossed the street. "Norma lives in your house."

Molly couldn't believe it. The girl she liked best, living right in her house. They could see each other all the time. Even if the weather was bad. Maybe God had heard her wish, after all.

"No kidding? What floor?" Molly asked, trying to keep the excitement out of her voice, so Celia wouldn't see how pleased she was.

"Third, in the back," Norma said.

"Then you can see my windows. I live on the ground floor, in the front," Molly said.

"If you come to the window, we can talk," Norma said.

Celia laughed. "She can see your window. From my house, I can look in her kitchen and see your window, too," she said.

When they got to Celia's stoop, Molly watched her go up the steps. She wasn't limping at all. Molly was about

to mention this to Norma when she noticed her mother in the window. She had been gone a long time. Her mother must have been worried. She should have said something.

Molly ran up to the window.

"Where were you?" her mother asked. "I was ready to call the police."

"I'm sorry, Ma," Molly said. But she was too full of news to explain just then. The events of the morning came tumbling out of her. "MaIwenttosummer schoolandIcameinsecondinthebeanbagraceandMrs. RicewasinchargeandMathisisNormashelivesupstairs," she said all in one breath.

"How do you do, Norma?" her mother said. "Can you look in our window, too?"

Molly smiled, glad her mother wasn't angry at her.

"We saw you move in, but we weren't looking," Norma said.

"Of course not," Molly's mother said. She turned to Molly. "I am keeping the baby in the house. He has a loose stomach. Rebecca's coming out. Keep an eye on her, please."

Molly could have spit. She didn't want Rebecca around, not now, when she had a new friend. She wished Rebecca could have had the loose stomach instead.

Molly turned to Norma. "Don't mind her," she said. "She won't bother us. She plays by herself."

54

"That's okay," Norma said. "I have to go up anyhow. My mother is strict. I have to go right home after summer school." She started up the steps. "I'll see you after lunch, Molly," she said, and went in.

Hearing Norma say her name made Molly feel warm all over. It was as though they were close friends already. What a difference between Norma and Celia, Molly thought, feeling happy. Nothing could take away her good feelings, not even Rebecca.

Molly noticed, as Rebecca came out, that one of her shoelaces was untied.

"Come here, and I'll tie your lace," she said.

"I don't want to," Rebecca said, heading for the side to hold on.

"See if I care," Molly said. "You'll trip and get a bloody nose."

The words did their magic. Rebecca lifted up her foot and let Molly tie the lace. Then she looked around for someone to play with. It was lunchtime, and all the children were indoors. Rebecca took hold of the side of the stoop, went down to the bottom step, sat down, and stuck the rag in her mouth.

Molly felt sorry for her sister. Anna was sitting on the stoop. And as a treat, Molly decided to take Rebecca across the street to meet her.

"Come on," she said, going down and offering her a hand. "You'll meet my first friend in the neighborhood."

Hand in hand, they went across the street.

"Hi," Molly said, looking up at Anna.

Anna had been staring off into space. She turned to face Molly.

"I went to the schoolyard today," Molly said. "I came in second in the bean-bag race."

Anna smiled.

"This is my little sister, Rebecca," Molly said.

Rebecca made a face and drew back.

"Say hello," Molly said, pushing her sister forward. Rebecca tried to smile, and shoved the rag in her mouth.

Anna put her hands to her head. Her face twisted and she began to cry suddenly. She made no sound, but tears ran down her cheeks.

"Let's go. I'm afraid," Rebecca said.

Molly felt a little afraid, too. Not because Anna might harm her. She was too kind for that. But Molly felt strange, seeing a grown-up cry.

"See you later," Molly said, taking Rebecca's hand and leading her to the curb. Molly wondered, as they crossed the street, if what Celia had said was true. Could it be possible? Was Anna crazy?

"The fat lady smells," Rebecca said when they reached the house.

Molly had noticed it, too. But she didn't like hearing Rebecca say so. "She does not. That was the garbage. The can was open," she said.

Mama came to the window.

"Molly, find Joey and tell him I have a job for him. Then we'll eat lunch," she said, and ducked back in.

Joey wasn't playing ball across the street and Molly had no idea where to look for him.

Rebecca let go of her hand and ran up to join a little boy who had come out of one of the houses in the row.

As Molly stood wondering where to look for her brother, Norma came out.

"My mother's sending me to the candy store for ice cream. We're celebrating," she said. "Can you come with me?"

"Sure," Molly said, delighted to see her new friend so soon again.

Molly found out, as they walked to the corner, that Norma didn't like Celia either. And she found out what Norma was celebrating. Her father was a pharmacist. The drugstore where he worked had closed down. And he had just found a new job—in Philadelphia.

"When will you see him?" Molly asked, thinking she wouldn't like it if her father weren't around.

"He'll come weekends. If he has to work, my mother and I will go there," Norma said.

That impressed Molly even further. Norma talked about going to Philadelphia as if it were nothing. Not even Molly's parents had been there yet.

She was surprised to see her brother in the candy store, sitting at the fountain and having an egg cream.

57

She had forgotten that she was supposed to be looking for him.

"Mama wants you," Molly said, going up to him.

He looked annoyed. "You spying or something?" he said.

"Mama told me to look for you," Molly said. "I didn't know you were here. I came in with my friend," she said, nodding down the counter at Norma.

Joey took two pennies out of his pocket and gave Molly one. "One for you, and one for Rebecca," he said. "A lady gave me a nickel tip for carrying her groceries."

"Thanks," Molly said, pleased at the unexpected treat. She looked around and decided not to spend her penny till after lunch.

"You coming, Molly?" Norma asked, standing with a container in her hand.

Molly heard her brother give the egg cream a final slurp through the straw as she went to join Norma.

5
Friday Night

Molly often thought of Selma and Faigl. But she was busy with her new friends and didn't have time to miss them as much as in the beginning.

Wednesday morning, she went back to the school-yard. All the same girls were there. This time, Julie was there, too. Molly was glad to see her again. They played all morning, first ball, then Chinese checkers. Then Molly played regular checkers with Norma. Then Mrs. Rice got a Bingo game going. The prize was a hi-li, and Little Naomi won it.

Celia disappeared after the game and Molly looked around for her. She and Norma and Julie had to laugh when they found her. Celia was hiding in a doorway, eating a chocolate bar by herself, so she wouldn't have to offer anyone a bite.

In the afternoon, Molly went to Julie's house with Norma. They didn't stay long. Julie's mother had had an attack and was walking around with a cold compress on her head. She said she couldn't stand the children's voices. So they went down and looked in the store windows on Thirteenth Avenue—Julie, too.

When they got home, Molly went up to Norma's house for the first time. She nearly *plotzed* when she saw it. Norma had her own room. They had a rug in the living room, not an oilcloth. But the biggest surprise of all was the telephone. Molly had seen telephones in candy stores. When her father used to work late, he used to leave a message in the candy store, and someone would go tell her mother. But she never knew a person could have a phone right in their own house!

On Thursday, Molly and Norma became best friends. They told each other, but promised to keep it secret from everyone else—especially Celia. She wanted to be everybody's best friend.

On Friday, it was almost as if Molly had never moved. She did all the things she had always done on Friday—she even got a book from the library. Norma took her there in the morning and she signed up for a new card. The librarian said she could take a book out on Norma's card, until hers arrived in the mail. The librarian then suggested Molly take out *Little Women*, but Molly looked at it and thought it was too hard. Instead, she took out *Pinocchio.* Norma had read it and said it was good.

After the library, she went to the movies with Shami and Little Naomi to buy a ticket for the Saturday afternoon show. They bought tickets in advance because their families were religious and they weren't allowed to carry money on the Sabbath. But they could present the ticket at the door on Saturday, and go in.

When she saw what was playing, she nearly jumped with joy. Shami had said a Fat-and-Skinny movie was on. Molly liked Abbott and Costello all right. But what was playing was a Bette Davis movie. And she was crazy about Bette Davis!

Afterwards, it was time to go home and help her mother make ready for the Sabbath. Molly hated to go in. It was always so much more interesting outside, on the street. But it was Friday—and her duties were waiting.

She put her movie ticket under the runner on her dresser, then helped. She polished the silver candlesticks that used to belong to her grandmother, she helped her mother change the bedding, and while her mother washed the kitchen floor she emptied the laundry bag and separated everybody's clothes. When the floor was washed, Molly spread newspapers out over it to keep it clean. Then she got out the white tablecloth and set the table, laying an extra plate for Aunt Bessie, Papa's sister, who always spent *Shabbos* with them.

She still had a couple of things to do but she decided they could wait. She wanted to go outside.

"I'm tired, Ma. I'll finish later," she said. Then, so as not to seem selfish, she added, "I'll go out for a while and watch Rebecca."

Her mother looked up from chopping fish in a

wooden bowl on the kitchen table. "How come you're being such an angel suddenly?" she asked.

Molly knew her mother was teasing. She teased back.

"Kidnappers might come," she said, with a smile.

"Ptu!" her mother said, making the sound of spitting. "Don't make such jokes."

Molly laughed, and went out.

The street was deserted, except for Anna. There was no sign of Rebecca, either. Molly wondered if Rebecca was with Mrs. Chiodo, the next-door neighbor. She was with Mrs. Chiodo a lot of the time.

Molly leaned over the side of the stoop. "Rebecca!" she called.

Mrs. Chiodo and Rebecca appeared in the window at the same moment. Molly noticed a piece of Italian bread in her sister's hand.

"Rebecca's here with me, don't worry," Mrs. Chiodo said.

"I just wondered," Molly said, and looked away.

She wished one of her friends would show up. She knew they were at home, helping their mothers, but she kept hoping to see one of them just the same. Across the street, the man who raised pigeons came to the edge of the roof with his long stick. Molly watched as he swung the stick around, calling the pigeons home.

After a while, she decided to go across the street and talk to Anna.

"Hi, Anna," Molly called up to Anna, who was staring off into space.

Anna turned slowly to her. Her eyes were half closed. She reached up with both hands and squeezed her head. "My head hurts me," she said.

"Take an aspirin," Molly said. She felt strange talking to Anna that way, as if she were the grown-up and Anna the child.

Anna suddenly wrapped her huge arms around herself and shivered. "It's cold," she said. "Put a sweater on."

Molly felt uncomfortable. She couldn't understand Anna. It was boiling hot out. "I'm not cold," she said, afraid to say more.

To her relief, Anna's mother came to the window.

"Anna, come up," she called.

Anna got up. She took a pistachio nut out of her pocket and held it out to Molly. Molly didn't like pistachio nuts, but she thanked her just the same as she reached up to take it. Anna went upstairs.

Molly examined the nut. She couldn't eat it if she wanted to. It was sealed all around. That's what she didn't like about those nuts. She put it in her pocket and headed back to the house.

As she crossed the street, she saw Rebecca walk out of Mrs. Chiodo's eating a cookie and go up the steps of the stoop.

Molly wondered if she should go in, too. It was getting close to the Sabbath. None of her friends would be coming out anymore. She decided to go in and read her new library book.

As she opened the door of the apartment, her mouth watered at the delicious Friday smells. The fish bubbled away on the stove and her mother, leaning over another pot, was tasting the chicken soup with a wooden spoon.

"Molly, make the table ready for *Shabbos*," her mother said.

Molly was irritated. She didn't have to be told. "I was just going to do that," she said.

She put the *challa* bread on the table and covered it with a doily. Then she brought the candlesticks to the table and put a box of kitchen matches beside them. At the moment of nightfall, her mother would light the candles to welcome the Sabbath.

Molly got her book from her room and went into the living room.

"Before you sit down, take out the bed for Bessie," her mother said.

"I was going to read!" Molly said.

"You'll read when you're finished."

Molly flung the book on the couch, then went into her room and rolled the folding bed out of the closet. That was where Bessie slept. Molly thought of her aunt and smiled. Bessie was big and fat and she laughed a lot. Her gold tooth was always flashing in her mouth. Molly looked forward to seeing her.

As she leaned over the bed to tuck in the sheet, the pistachio nut fell out of her pocket. She was about to throw it out the window, then decided not to. Though it was only a nut, it was a present from Anna, her first friend. Molly put the nut in her drawer, then went back to the living room.

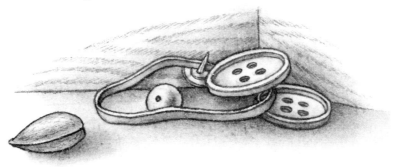

"Pick up the newspapers," her mother called in.

"Ma!" Molly said, stamping her foot.

"Afterwards you'll sit down."

Annoyed, Molly picked the newspapers up from the nice and clean floor and threw them in the garbage, then went back into the living room.

"I'm going to read now," she said, standing in front of the couch, daring her mother to stop her.

Her mother had no further requests to make of her, so she sat down and opened her book. It was about a boy made of wood. At first she didn't like it. It was too easy. But as she read on she became interested. He was a liar and foolish and he kept getting into trouble.

She heard the radio go on in the kitchen and her mother say to Rebecca, "Not now, Molly's reading," but she read on, annoyed that the father should sell his one and only jacket to buy his son a spelling book, and that that ungrateful Pinocchio should run away.

She was aware when her father and Joey left for the synagogue and she could ignore all the familiar sounds in the kitchen as she read, but when she heard her Aunt Bessie's voice, she put her book down and ran inside.

Going up to her aunt, Molly threw her arms around her and squeezed.

"My fingers don't touch," she said, trying to get her fingers to meet.

Her aunt looked down. *"Oy vay!"* she said, pretending to be shocked. "Don't tell me I got fatter."

Molly laughed. They did the same thing every Friday, yet Bessie always managed to sound surprised.

"I think you did," Molly said, teasing.

"No, she didn't," Rebecca said. "She's the same fat as before."

"I think Rebecca's right," Bessie said.

"Oh, she doesn't know anything, she's only a baby," Molly said.

Rebecca looked like she was getting ready to start up and Mama made a face to Molly to say no more.

"There's only one baby in this house, and he's sleeping," she said, giving Molly a wink.

Bessie reached into her shopping bag and handed Mama a loaf of bread and a box of salt.

"For the new house," she said. "Bread for life, and salt to give spice to the life."

Mama thanked Bessie and put the things away.

66

"And this is for Rebecca," Bessie said, giving her a wooden duck on wheels that could be pulled.

"Is it new?" Rebecca asked, looking the duck over.

"Almost," Bessie said.

Rebecca put the duck on the floor and pulled it away.

"The boss let me off early today," Bessie said to Mama. "So I went to see Remerke."

"Goody," Molly said. Remerke was Papa's rich cousin. All Molly's clothes were hand-me-downs from Remerke's daughter. "Did they send me something to wear when school starts?"

"You could wear it, but you might get arrested," Bessie said, handing her a pair of flannel pajamas.

Molly took it and made a face. "They're for winter," she said. "Besides, they're too big."

"Never mind big, you'll grow into them," Mama said. "And you'll be glad to have them when winter comes."

Molly left her mother and aunt talking in the kitchen and went into her room to put the pajamas away. Then she returned to the living room and picked up her book again. She plunged right into the story. That wooden kid's nose grew when he lied. She wondered what he was up to.

"*Gottenyu!*" Molly heard her mother cry.

Frightened, Molly sat up. That sound could only mean trouble. Were they talking about Hitler? Had he killed more Jews? She tried to listen, but the voices in the kitchen had grown dim and she couldn't hear what they were saying. Molly read on.

"It's time to light the candles," her mother called.

Molly got up and went into the kitchen. Mama and Bessie were standing at the table with kerchiefs thrown over their heads. Molly remembered last Friday and smiled. Mama couldn't find her kerchief and she grabbed Papa's hat and used that as a head covering.

"Remember what Mama did last week?" Molly asked, with a smile.

"So what? So long as the head is covered," Bessie said.

"So long as the head is covered," Mama repeated. "Rebecca, I'm waiting," she called.

Rebecca came strolling out of Joey's room, sucking the rag and pulling the duck along.

Molly looked at her sister. That rag was always in her mouth.

"Ma," she asked, "when is Rebecca going to stop sucking that thing?"

"When she's sixteen," Mama said.

"Come on, Ma," Molly said, annoyed. "Why can't you give me a straight answer?"

"Come on, what?" her mother asked. "I'm sure when she's sixteen, she won't be doing it anymore. What can be straighter than that?"

Rebecca took the rag out of her mouth and gave Molly a smile, showing her tiny teeth.

Mama struck a match and lit the candles.

"Quiet, children," Bessie said.

"*Boruch atoh Adonai*," Mama began. "Blessed art thou, O Lord, our God, King of the Universe, who hast hallowed us by thy commandments, and commanded us to kindle the Sabbath lights."

Then she praised God and asked the Lord to bless everyone in the family and to protect the relatives in Europe and please—please to stop Hitler from killing Jews.

Bessie silently said her own prayer.

Molly looked at the flickering candles. She loved this moment. The house always felt different when the candles were lit. The clean floors—the good smells in the kitchen—the dancing flames. It was *Shabbos*, a holy day, a day of pleasure and rest.

Soon Papa and Joey were home from the synagogue and everyone sat down to eat. Papa removed the doily from the *challa* bread and said a blessing over it. He gave everyone a piece and each person said his and her own blessing. Mama took out the chopped chicken liver. Then she and Bessie brought the soup to the table, and the *Shabbos* dinner, the best meal of the week, was underway.

"No carrots," Rebecca said as Mama put a spoonful of *tsimmes* on her plate.

With a fork, Mama separated the carrots from the meat and prunes and potatoes and put them on Joey's plate.

"Thanks," Joey said. "Any other contributions?"

"He'll eat anything," Molly said to no one in particular, and dug in.

"*Nu,*" Mama said to Bessie, "are you going to tell your brother what happened?"

Papa looked at Bessie. "What happened?"

"I went to see the cousins today," she said.

"And? How are they?"

"Abrasha's sick again."

"I'm sorry to hear it."

Molly asked Joey for the ketchup and poured some on her plate.

"I didn't mean about the cousins," Mama said.

"I know, I know," Bessie said.

Papa glanced from Mama to Bessie. "Is somebody going to tell me what happened, or not?"

Bessie finished chewing, then turned to her brother. "I got laid off today," she said.

Molly looked up. Then it wasn't Hitler they were talking about before. Bessie had lost her job.

"There's no work," Bessie explained. "Ladies don't wear hats anymore. The boss had to close down the shop."

Papa looked down at his plate. Molly knew what he was thinking. She had heard the questions asked before. How would Bessie pay her rent? How would she buy food? Would she have to go on relief?

"God will help," Papa said, and took a mouthful of food.

Bessie licked her lips. "The *tsimmes* is delicious, better than last week."

"Wait till you taste the fish tomorrow," Mama said.

After a few moments, everyone was eating and talking again. Bessie told a funny story about a lady at work, a greenhorn who had just come to America from the Other Side, putting cherries instead of feathers on a hat a woman had ordered. Everyone laughed. Molly knew the worries were still there, underneath, but for now there were joyful sounds again and she was glad.

Molly heard her name called in the courtyard and ran to the window. She looked up to see Norma.

"Can you come up?" Norma asked.

Putting a finger to her lips, Molly shushed her and pointed to Celia's window. If Celia heard, she would only want to come, too.

"We're still eating," Mama said from the table. "Let her come down, if she wants."

Molly signaled Norma to come down instead and Norma nodded that she would.

Molly went back to the table.

"Why didn't you tell her to come down?" Mama asked.

"I did," Molly said.

Mama gave her a questioning look, then got up and brought the stewed fruit to the table. As she gave everyone some dessert in little glass cups, Papa began to sing a table hymn. Joey slid a cup of fruit over to himself, and joined in. Soon everyone around the table was singing.

Molly felt sorry for Bessie. And she felt sorry for the Jews of Europe. And she wished that rotten Hitler would drop dead. But for now, everyone was singing, and her best friend was on her way down the stairs, and she couldn't help but feel happy.

6
The Funeral

Molly, Celia, Julie, and Norma sat on Molly's stoop talking. They began a game of jacks, but started to talk about school instead. September was coming and the subject was very much on Molly's mind. She could hardly think of anything else. Her friends went to P.S. 164 and knew all about it. But she had never been there before and she couldn't stop asking questions about her new school.

Norma's mother had bought her a new skirt to wear. Celia and Julie had new outfits, too. Molly silently wished she had something other than her lucky dress to wear on the first day of school.

"I wonder who's going to be sitting next to me," she said.

"Come on, I'm tired of this subject," Celia said. She picked up the jacks. "Let's play. I'll go first."

"No," Molly said. "We'll choose who goes first."

"Okay, I'll say it, then," Celia said.

74

Everyone stuck out a fist as Celia recited:

"Ink, a-bink, a bottle of ink,
The cork fell out and you stink."

She tapped every fist, including her own, as she said the words, and the last word landed on Julie.

"I'm first," Julie said. "After my turn, I'll give the jacks to whoever I want to."

Molly knew she meant those words for Celia. Julie had changed toward Celia. She wasn't afraid of her anymore. She still couldn't say "Celia" to her face. But she didn't call her Lynn anymore either.

Julie scooped up the jacks and began to play.

Molly couldn't help herself. She just had to know more. "I wonder who is going to be in my class," she said, watching the ball bounce and the jacks scatter.

"Hmmm," Julie said, her eye on the ball.

"Me, too," Norma said.

"Oh, who cares?" Celia said. "I hate regular school. Give me summer school anytime."

No matter how many times Molly heard Celia say that, she was always surprised. She couldn't understand how anyone could feel that way about school when there was so much of interest going on there—the teachers, the subjects, the other children.

Julie finished her turn and handed Norma the ball.

"I wonder if I'm going to get Miss Slattery," Molly

75

said. "Big Naomi said Miss Slattery was mean."

"She is not," Julie said. "I like her."

"She is, too, mean. She's the meanest teacher in the whole school," Celia said.

"How would you know? You never had her," Julie said.

Celia looked daggers at Julie. "I know, that's how!" she said.

No one spoke. Julie looked away. Celia had that look on her face that made everything come to a stop. Molly hated to admit it to herself, but sometimes Celia reminded her of her sister Rebecca. She was glad to see her mother come to the window.

"Molly, come in. I'm going out," her mother said.

Molly got up. Her mother had to go someplace. And she would have to mind the baby. He had a loose stomach again, and it was better for him to stay inside. Molly wished Norma would come with her, but she made no move to get up. They were still best friends. But Norma had been going to Philadelphia a lot lately—sometimes leaving with her mother in the morning and returning in the evening.

"I have to go in," Molly said. "I'll talk to you from the window." As she looked up, she saw Rebecca chasing after a little boy. "Rebecca, don't go near the gutter," Molly called, and went inside.

Mama was waiting at the door, her pocketbook under her arm. "If the baby cries, give him the bottle. I'll be back soon," she said.

"Where are you going, anyhow?" Molly asked, realizing she didn't know.

"To see Mrs. Orenstein."

Molly made a face. Some of her parents' old-fashioned ways embarrassed her. Mrs. Orenstein found husbands and wives for people who wanted to get married.

"Wait a minute!" Molly said, realizing suddenly why her mother was going there. It was on account of Aunt Bessie. She had heard her parents talking about her the other night.

"Are you going to get a husband for Aunt Bessie?" Molly asked, showing off that she knew.

"No, for you. I'm tired of having you around the house," her mother said.

"Ma! Stop it!" Molly said, and she stamped her foot.

"I stopped. I am going."

Her mother opened the door and went out.

Molly ran to the front window. She sat on her knees, on the couch, and looked out. Big Naomi had joined her other friends and she said hello. She watched her mother go up to Rebecca, then head down the street.

Celia jumped up. "What are we waiting for? Let's go," she said.

"Where are you going?" Molly asked, seeing everyone get up.

Big Naomi held out her hand and showed Molly a quarter.

"My uncle gave it to me, just to spend," she said.

"We're going to Thirteenth Avenue to get Italian ices."

Norma laughed. "It better be a big one. Everyone is going for a lick."

"I don't want a lick," Celia said. "I'm going just to walk Julie home."

Like fun, Molly thought. Celia would end up getting Naomi to buy her something all for herself, and something that cost more than a penny, too.

"Come on," Celia said, pulling Big Naomi along.

Molly watched them go, then turned away. She glanced sourly at the bedroom, where the baby was asleep. If not for him, she would be going with them. She got her book from the kitchen, where she had left it, and sat down on the couch, in front of the open window, to read.

The book she was reading was *Heidi.* It took her a moment or two to get started, on account of the sounds in the street. But she concentrated on the words and soon she was all caught up in the story of Heidi, a little Swiss girl who was sent to live with her grandfather in the mountains. Suddenly a fearful noise from the street roused her and she swung around on her knees to look out.

A horse was slowly pulling a black wagon. Men and women all dressed in black walked behind, crying and moaning, some screaming and beating their chests. Molly shuddered. Chills ran up and down her spine. Worried about her sister, she looked to see where she was. Rebecca stood watching the strange sight. She looked up at Molly and burst into tears. Then she came running up the stoop.

Molly ran to open the door for her. She was as frightened as her sister, but she pretended not to be.

"What are you crying for?" Molly asked.

Rebecca could hardly speak. Sobbing, she pointed outside.

Molly tried to smile. "It's only a horse," she said.

"No-o-ooo!" Rebecca yelled.

It hurt Molly to see her sister so upset. She picked Rebecca up in her arms and held her as best she could. "Shhh," she said, "the baby is sleeping." She rocked her sister gently. "You want a glass of milk?" she asked.

"N-no," Rebecca said.

"A cookie?"

Rebecca shook her head.

"Do you want me to read to you?"

Rebecca nodded.

"Will you stop crying?"

Rebecca nodded again.

"Promise?"

"Uh-huh," Rebecca said through her tears.

Molly carried her sister into the living room and sat down with her on the couch. They could still hear the cries and moans, but the sounds were further away and more blurry now. Molly opened her book and put it face up in Rebecca's lap.

"Don't cry on it and get it wet," she said.

"I won't."

Molly put one arm around her sister and turned the pages with her other hand. She wondered, as she read aloud, how Rebecca could follow the story. She hadn't heard the beginning. Yet she sat listening to every word, waiting for Molly to turn the page.

"Ma!" Molly cried, hearing the door open and seeing her mother standing there. "You should have seen what was in the street before."

Molly realized too late that she shouldn't have said anything. Rebecca started to cry all over again. Mama picked her up and kissed her.

"*Shah, shah, mein kind,*" Mama said, stroking Rebecca. "I saw it, too. . . ."

"What was it, Ma?" Molly asked.

"Ptu!" Mama said, spitting the thought away. "A funeral. May we not know from such things."

The word chilled Molly. "Ma, it was terrible. It scared Rebecca," she said.

"It could scare anyone," Mama said, half to herself. Rebecca had stopped crying. Mama glanced at her and saw that she was half asleep. "Not all funerals are like that," she added softly. "In the old country, the orthodox people, they have funerals like that."

She looked at Molly. "I'm home now. So why don't you go out?"

82

Molly didn't feel like going out. "I don't want to," she said.

"Go," Mama repeated. "Celia's outside."

"Big Naomi, too?" Molly asked.

"Big Naomi, Little Naomi, the whole bunch," Mama said.

Molly was sure Celia had talked Big Naomi into buying her something. She went out to see for herself. Her friends were standing in front of Celia's house. "Hmmph," Molly said to herself, going up to them. She was right. Everyone was eating from a bag of candy that Big Naomi held open. But Celia—she had a lollipop that cost two cents all to herself. Molly despised Celia in that moment.

"Did you see the funeral?" Molly asked.

"Ugh!" Norma said, making a face. "Yeah, we saw it."

Little Naomi gave a shiver. "It's still there"—she nodded toward the corner—"by the synagogue."

Molly sensed that her friends were as frightened as she was. "It scared Rebecca," she said. "She was crying like anything."

"Poo!" Celia said. "Who cares? She was crazy, anyhow."

"Who?" Molly asked.

"Fat Anna, that's who. It was her funeral!"

Molly felt dizzy suddenly. Big Naomi shoved the bag of candy under her nose. "Take one," she said. "There's jelly beans, too."

Molly shook her head. "I have to go in," she said.

"She's just jealous she didn't go with us," she heard Celia say as she went up the steps.

Molly didn't care what Celia said. She wasn't jealous. It wasn't that at all. She had never known anyone who had died before. Now someone she knew was dead. Was gone. Forever.

Staring down at an open book, pretending to be reading, Molly thought of death. She saw herself at her mother's funeral, at her father's funeral, at Aunt Bessie's. Then she saw her own funeral, with everyone walking behind and crying, and almost scared herself to death.

She was glad to get up when her mother called her into the kitchen for supper.

"Tell us what's wrong," Papa said again, at the supper table.

"Nothing," Molly said, staring down at her plate.

"Tell us," Mama said, from the stove.

Molly looked up. "I told you a hundred times, nothing! I just want to be left alone."

"All she wants is attention," Joey said, shaking the ketchup bottle over his boiled potato.

Her brother had been getting on her nerves all evening. "Drop dead!" she said, and was instantly sorry.

"Children!" Mama said. "I won't have such language in my house." She looked from one to the other. "Joey,"

84

she added, "tonight you'll dry, too."

Joey looked up. "Me? I wash, Molly dries."

"Tonight you'll do both," Mama said.

Joey turned to Papa. "Pa!"

"You heard Mama," Papa said.

Mama's thoughtfulness made Molly feel better. After supper, she went into the living room to read. Papa was out at a meeting of the Jewish War Veterans. Mama and Joey were in the kitchen, listening to the radio. Molly put down her book to listen to the news. The announcer said that in Rumania Jewish boys and girls were forced into labor camps. Their parents had been taken away.

Molly sighed. That meant the parents were killed. Dead. Like Anna. Molly wanted to cry.

She put her book away and got ready for bed. Rebecca was fast asleep. Molly quietly slid open the dresser drawer and took out the pistachio nut Anna had given her. She put it under her pillow as she got into bed.

She was tired but she could not fall asleep. She heard Joey say good night. She heard her mother go into the living room and open the couch. The baby woke up and began to cry. She listened to her mother sing, softly, gently, "Ai-lu-lu-lu, baby. Sleep, Mama's pretty baby."

The lullaby soothed Molly and her eyes began to grow heavy. She dozed, but did not fall asleep. She heard her father come home. Then she heard him get into bed. She listened to her parents talking.

"*Nu?* Did you find out what was bothering her?" Papa said.

"I met Mrs. Leibowitz in the hall when I went to take out the garbage," Mama said. "She told me Celia's mother was moving. That's probably why she's acting that way. Celia is her best friend."

Molly's eyes flew open. Celia! Her best friend? She hated Celia! That's how much parents understood about children. She reached under the pillow and closed her fingers over the pistachio nut. She thought of Anna, her first friend, and remembered the last time she saw her. "It's cold," Anna had said. "Put a sweater on." Molly had to smile to herself. It was boiling hot out. She would have roasted in a sweater.

The sweater reminded her of school, and she thought of the new pencil box she bought in the five-and-ten, of the schoolbag she had inherited from Norma, and of all the nice brown paper she was smoothing out every day, to make covers with, and of how neat and clean her books were going to look with nice brown covers over them.

Her fingers loosened around the nut and after a while she fell asleep.

7

New Neighbors

Molly had been moping around the house all morning, feeling sorry for herself. She had no one to play with. All her friends seemed to have disappeared suddenly. School was still a week away. But for some reason, they were all staying home more, as if school had already started.

What was bothering her even more was that Norma was in Philadelphia again. She was there more and more now. Last night, she had told Molly that she might be moving there for good.

"Why don't you take a book and read?" her mother asked.

"I just finished a book," Molly said.

"Start another one."

"I'm saving it," Molly said.

She leaned out the living-room window and looked around. No one she knew was out there. Just Rebecca and her friends. She went into the kitchen and ate a banana. Then she *kootsie-kooed* the baby for a while. When she got tired of that, she decided to start on a new book, after all. Luckily, she had taken three out of the library on Friday. She would still have one left for later in the week.

She looked the two books over and decided on the Nancy Drew. It was a mystery, and easy to read. She envied Nancy her interesting life. Nancy's father was a lawyer. And Nancy helped him solve all his cases.

The thought of starting a new story began to excite her. She could even have the room to herself, for a change, with Rebecca out of the house.

"I'm going into my room to read," Molly called to her mother, and closed the door.

She sat down on the bed, opened the book, and began to read. The emerald necklace of old Mrs. Rogers, the rich lady who lived on the hill, had been stolen. Nancy and her friends were talking about it, wondering who could have done it.

Molly read on, lost in the story, until her aunt arrived and Heshy's booming voice exploded in the living room. She put the book down. Heshy was the man Mrs. Orenstein had found for Aunt Bessie to marry. Molly made a face. She found the whole thing unpleasant. Her aunt was too old to be getting married. And Heshy was pretty awful.

Not only was his loud voice getting on her nerves, but the smell of his cigar was, too. It came through the door.

Annoyed, Molly got up. There was no use trying to read. She might as well go sit outside where at least the air was fresh.

She opened the door to the living room. Her mother and aunt were sitting on the couch, in front of the window. Heshy was in the easy chair, puffing on his cigar and talking. Molly would have liked to ignore him. But her mother would only yell at her later for having been rude.

"Hi," she said, glancing past Heshy at the radio.

Before she knew it, she was sitting in the living room. Heshy had jumped up, pulled a chair in from the kitchen, and practically shoved her into it.

Molly was furious with herself. Why had she let him push her down? She didn't want to be sitting there with the old folks. And she certainly didn't want to be listening to him. She should have said she had to go someplace. Or that her friends were waiting for her. Anything. Now he was talking, and she was stuck. She couldn't figure out a way to get up and leave.

She coughed as Heshy took another puff on his cigar and began talking about his favorite subject—Poland, the place where he was born. Molly closed off her nose and tried to breathe through her mouth. How could her mother and aunt stand the stink? She looked at them, sitting on the couch and smiling. Molly rolled her eyes. Heshy was telling how he had saved up enough money to come to America. Even she had heard that story before.

Molly was sick not only of Heshy, but of her aunt, too. Her aunt had changed since she met Heshy. She acted stupid when he was around, nodding and smiling all the time, with her greenhorn gold tooth showing.

Molly was annoyed at her mother, too. Was she blind? Couldn't she see how bored her daughter was? Why didn't she help, and send her outside to play? Molly stared at her mother, trying to force her to notice how miserable she was.

"Yes, sir," Heshy said, "the best air in the world is in Coney Island."

Oy, Molly thought, there he goes again. Coney Island was his second favorite subject. He was a waiter in a restaurant on the boardwalk there.

He took another puff on his cigar. Molly coughed again, and opened her mouth a crack at the side to blow away the smoke. She stared over her mother's head, out the window, wishing she had some of that good Coney Island air to breathe right now.

A moment later, to her great joy, she saw a moving van pull up at the curb. At last! Now she had an excuse.

"There's the truck," she cried, jumping up, as if she had been waiting for it. "My friend is moving—I have to say good-bye."

Before a word could be said, she ran into the kitchen, deposited her book on top of the icebox, found her rubber-band ball bag, and ran out.

"Whew!" she said, standing on the stoop. Earlier, she

had complained to her mother that she had no one to play with. Now she was glad to find herself alone. She breathed deeply, filling her lungs with air. This Borough Park air is as good as Coney Island air anytime, she thought.

She sat down and took out her ball. It was finished. She could make it bigger, if she wanted to, but it was big enough. She felt its hardness, and bounced it a couple of times to see how high it went. It bounced easily and she went down to the sidewalk to try it out. Starting with the first letter of the alphabet, she began to play A, My Name Is. . . .

She stopped to watch the two movers carry a couch out next door.

Good riddance, she thought, and wondered who would be moving into Celia's house next. The idea intrigued her, and she went back up on the stoop and sat down to think about it.

It seemed to her that people were always moving. Why couldn't they stay in one place? she wondered. She thought about Selma, her first best friend. She hated to admit it to herself, but she couldn't remember what Selma looked like anymore. She remembered how she used to feel about her, and some of the things they did together, and her ponytail, but not her face. Her face had faded away.

Molly closed her eyes and hoped there would be a girl her own age moving in next door, someone she could become friendly with. As she glanced up, she saw her brother coming out of a house across the street. He was with a boy she had never seen before. Molly wondered if he was new. Or if he was one of the rich kids on the block who had been away for the summer. The rich people went to the mountains for the summer.

The boys came walking up to her.

"This is my sister," Joey said.

"Hi, I'm Solly," the boy said.

"I'm Molly," Molly said, with a laugh. They all laughed.

"Heshy's in there," Molly said, nodding toward the window.

"Thanks for the warning." Joey turned to Solly. "We can't go in, unless you want to hear about the wonderful air in Coney Island," he said.

Solly smiled as if he understood.

"Come on," Joey said. "Somebody in the schoolyard is bound to have a ball."

"You want this one?" Molly asked, holding up her ball.

"Naaa, somebody can get killed with that," her brother said, running down the steps.

Molly watched them go, then returned to her thoughts about who might be moving in next door. She pictured a small girl, about her own size, who would be in her class, and who would sit next to her in the front of the room, with the other small kids. She pictured them walking to school together. And pictured them whispering in class, and trying not to get caught, then walking home from school together. She let herself dream about her new friend, and in her mind saw herself and her friend together a lot.

When she looked up again, she saw the movers lock the back of the truck and get into the front seat. Shortly, Celia, her mother, and the boarder came out. Celia's mother got into the front seat with the movers. Celia got in and sat on her mother's lap. There was no room for the boarder. He waved good-bye to them and walked off.

As the truck pulled away, Celia's mother waved to Molly. Surprised, Molly waved back. Mrs. Bloch had never even spoken to her. Molly saw Mrs. Bloch poke Celia to wave, and saw Celia shove her mother's hand away. Molly was just as glad. Now she didn't have to wonder whether to wave or not. Double good riddance, she thought as the truck drove away.

Molly felt fidgety. She thought about going to Julie's house, then changed her mind. Julie's mother was a pill. She didn't like Julie's friends around. And she walked around moaning and with a cold towel on her head, trying to get them to leave.

As she thought about it, she saw that she could sneak back into the house and read. If she crept along the kitchen wall, she could get her book and run into Joey's room without being seen.

She got up and went inside, and nearly gagged as she opened the door. The kitchen was full of cigar smoke. The entire house stank now. She held her nose as she crept along the wall. Her mother saw her but said nothing. Soon Molly was in Joey's room, closing the door behind herself.

Her mother had rolled up the mattress, to air out the bed. Molly sat down on the springs, with her back against the mattress and her legs stretched out in front of herself. She opened her book.

Nancy Drew knew who the crook was. And she and her friends jumped into her red roadster and drove off to the old lady's house, to look for fingerprints on her vase.

Molly read on, lost to her surroundings, aware only of the red roadster zipping through town. After a while, the bedsprings began to pinch, and as she shifted she thought she saw movement in Celia's old windows. Curious, she looked up. Two blond boys were staring down at her.

Embarrassed, Molly jumped off the bed. Was it possible that new people had moved in already? She stepped to the side, where she could see without being seen, and looked out. The boys were gone. But new people had definitely moved in. A woman was hanging curtains at the window. Molly couldn't wait to find out if there was a girl in the family, too.

She hurried into the bathroom. Unbelievably, Heshy

was still talking. Molly washed her face and hands, then studied herself in the mirror. She wondered how she would look in bangs. Bette Davis had worn them in the movie. Not long ones that went all the way across, but little bangs, off to one side.

Molly found a pair of scissors in the medicine chest. Then she parted her hair, and cut. When she was through, she found the bangs weren't even. She snipped some more. At last she was satisfied.

She examined herself in the mirror, first full face, then from the side. The bangs made her look more like Bette Davis. They made her look older, too. She wet the bangs to make them lie flat. Then, pleased with herself, she went out.

She seated herself so she could watch the neighboring stoop. She was ready to wait all day if she had to. Sooner or later, one of the new people had to come out. Molly closed her eyes and again pictured a girl coming out on the stoop next door, and waving to her. A new thought occurred to her and she opened her eyes wide.

She hoped the new family was Jewish. It would be easier to be friends if they were. They would understand each other's ways. It was also safer. The Irish and Italian kids picked on the Jewish kids.

Molly sat up straight. Her patience had been rewarded. One of the boys went running down the steps, heading for the corner. He was old, older than Joey. Molly wished she had said hello, but he was moving too fast. She got her voice ready for when he came back. But she didn't have to wait that long. A moment later, the other boy came out. He was younger, she could tell, as he stood glancing about.

"Hi," he called over to her. "That was you in the window before, wasn't it?"

Surprised, she nodded. How could he have recognized her? She looked so different with the bangs.

"Bennie—that's my brother—went to buy food," he said. "We have nothing to eat in the house." He turned and waved toward the corner. "My brother said that big building there must be the school."

"It is," Molly said, pleased to be in a position to give information.

"How is it?" he asked.

"I don't know." Molly smiled. "We just moved in, too, in July. I never went yet. I start in September."

"That makes two of us," he said.

Molly nodded, feeling pleased.

"Me and my brother came first, with my mother. My father's coming with the furniture."

Now was the time to ask, Molly thought. "Do you have a sister?"

He shook his head. "Only me and my brother," he said.

Molly was disappointed.

"I have a girl cousin, though," he added. "She comes over every Friday, her and her mother. They sleep over." Molly took that as good news. Then he had to be Jewish. If his cousin came on Fridays, it could only mean she was coming to spend *Shabbos* with his family.

"I'm in the sixth term," he said. "Maybe we'll be in the same class."

Molly beamed. He had taken her for older. It had to be the bangs, she thought.

"My brother Joey is in the sixth," she said." I'm starting fifth." She did not tell him she had skipped one term. He would have known how old she was and thought she was a baby.

He turned and saw his brother coming, and ran down the street to take the bag of groceries from him. The brother returned to the corner.

The boy glanced over at Molly as he carried the bag up the stoop. "He had to go get more things. See you later, alligator," he said, kicking the door open and going inside.

Molly was beside herself with joy. He had spoken to her as if she were a real person, not the way Joey and his friends did. So what if he was a boy? Boys could be friends, too. Besides, he had a girl cousin. Molly wished she knew his name. She should have asked. But she could ask him the next time she saw him, now that they were friends.

The old happiness that made her want to skip and sing slowly crept over her. It was not big enough to

98

make her want to skip, but she did want to sing. She pulled up her knees and wrapped her arms around her legs, getting ready to sing her happiness song. But just as she was about to begin, Mrs. Chiodo's door opened and Rebecca came walking out.

Annoyed, Molly dropped her legs over the side and sat up. She noticed, as Rebecca came up the steps, that her mouth was all red. Rebecca had been eating Mrs. Chiodo's spaghetti again! She wasn't allowed to do that. Mrs. Chiodo's food wasn't kosher. Another time, Molly would have let her sister have it. Now she wanted to get rid of her in a hurry, so she could go back to her good feeling.

"Better wipe the red off your mouth before Mama sees," Molly said.

Rebecca licked her lips clean, and went inside. Molly couldn't believe it. Now Heshy and Bessie came walking out. Molly was determined not to let anything spoil her good feeling. She smiled at Heshy's dumb jokes and let him muss her hair. And she put up with her aunt's good-bye hugs and kisses. She would have put up with anything, just to see them on their way. She watched them head, arm in arm, for the subway, then swung her legs back up on the stoop. Just as she was about to sit back, her mother came to the window.

Molly could have spit. Why couldn't she be left alone?

"Molly, guess what?" her mother said.

Molly was sure it was about the spaghetti on Rebecca's face. "About what?" she asked, playing dumb.

"Guess," her mother said, with a grin.

Molly saw from the expression on her mother's face that it wasn't about Rebecca. But if she was making her guess, it had to be something good, something worth guessing about. Could it be about the new neighbors? she wondered. Did her mother know something about them? Suddenly, Molly was curious.

"I don't want to guess, tell me," she said.

"Come on," her mother said.

"Tell me!" Molly said, impatiently.

Her mother was grinning from ear to ear. "Molly," she said, "Bessie is getting married."

Molly stared at her mother. Was that something to make her guess about? "Big deal!" she said, disappointed in the news. "I thought it was going to be something important."

She watched her mother's expression change. "Molly," her mother said, staring at her, "what did you do to yourself?"

Molly's heart began to pound. What had her mother seen? Was she bleeding?

"What happened to your head?" her mother asked.

Alarmed, Molly reached up to feel her head, expecting to find blood. "What is it?" she asked, worried.

"Your hair—" her mother said.

Molly had forgotten about the bangs. She could see

her mother didn't approve. "I like them even if you don't," Molly said. She spit on her fingertips and twisted the bangs into spit curls. "I'm sick of looking like a baby," she said.

Her mother only shook her head. "Come in and see what Bessie brought you from the cousins," she said. "She went there with Heshy this morning."

Molly was torn. She wanted to stay outside and get

back to her good feeling. But she was also curious about what Bessie had brought. She decided to go in and see, then come back out again.

Molly couldn't believe her eyes. Bessie's shopping bag was full of really nice things. Not dumb party dresses or camp clothes that she couldn't wear, but beautiful school clothes. Her mother and sister watched as she held up a white guimpe and a middy blouse with blue stars on the collar. But best of all was the navy-blue jumper with pleats, like the rich girls wore! Molly hugged the jumper to herself. God had rewarded her. She had something new to wear on the first day of school!

"It's beautiful," her mother said.

"Oh, Ma, it really is," Molly said.

As she stood in front of the mirror admiring how she looked with the jumper held up to herself, the baby started to cry, Rebecca took the duck for a walk across the floor, *quack-quack*ing to herself, and Mrs. Bloom was yelling to Mama to come to the courtyard window. Molly felt her good feeling slipping away. She was afraid that if she did not go out at once she would lose it forever.

"It's too noisy in here," she said to no one in particular. She hung the jumper up in the closet, next to her lucky dress, and went out.

Molly stood on the stoop trying to make herself quiet. The noise had spoiled her mood a little. She wanted to recapture her good feeling. She lowered her lids and glanced around. Two old ladies were returning from Thirteenth Avenue with shopping bags. Otherwise the street was empty. That was good. The quiet would help her find her way back inside herself, to the good feeling.

She sat down with her back against the wall. Moving slowly, trying to hold on to the quiet, she pulled up her knees and wrapped her arms around them. Now what were the thoughts that had led to the good feeling in the first place? She tried to remember. The new bangs, the new boy next door, his cousin who came on Fridays.

The good feeling was beginning to stir, she could feel it. To help it come back, she thought about school. That was her favorite thing to think about now. The new term started in a week and she could hardly wait for it to begin. By some miracle, she now had something new to wear. She smiled to herself, picturing herself in the white middy blouse with the blue stars on the collar, and the blue jumper with the kick pleats.

She pictured herself entering the classroom and the teacher calling to her to come and sit in the front row, near her. She pictured a girl sitting down next to her, and felt the girl would become her best friend—in case Norma did move. She saw herself carrying the books she had covered so neatly with the brown paper she had been saving, and saw herself going skating after school with the girl who sat next to her.

It was back! The good feeling was back. Her happiness song was bursting to come out. She rested her head on her knees and closed her eyes. She glanced up briefly, asking God to forgive her for feeling so good when Jews were being killed. She promised to worry about that later. For now, she was bursting with song.

Hugging herself tightly, squeezing, squeezing, she sang joyously, but so only she could hear,

"I should worry, I should care,
I should marry a millionaire."

Format by Gloria Bressler
Set in 12 point Gael
Composed, and bound by The Haddon Craftsmen, Inc.
Printed by The Murray Printing Co.

HARPER & ROW, PUBLISHERS, INCORPORATED